JUST LEAVE

NOT GOOD

RL

IT IS WHAT IT IS

STAY AWAY

SCRAM

UGH

PUKE

YUCK

BLAH

I'VE SEEN BETTER

LATER GATOR

TO MY STEP-MAMA HOLLY MAXSON,
WHO CRANKS OUT THE LOVE IN SPITE OF ALL CRANKINESS.
~SB

FOR LEAH.
THANK YOU TO KATELYN LIZARDI FOR HELPING
WITH COLORING WORK.
~DS

THE FOLLOWING MONSTERS CONTRIBUTED TO THE MAKING OF THIS BOOK:

AUTHOR: SAMANTHA "SAMOOCHES" BERGER
ILLUSTRATOR: DAN "WHAT A MIGHTY GOOD DAN" SANTAT
EDITORS: CONNIE "I HEART HSU" HSU, LIZA "EASY ON THE EYES-A" BAKER,
AND LESLIE "SHMOOPIE" SHUMATE
ART DIRECTOR: DAVE "LOVE TO LOVE YOU, DAVEY" CAPLAN
DESIGNER: MAGGIE "THAT'S WHAT *HE* SAID-KINS" EDKINS
PRODUCTION MANAGER: ERIKA "EVERMORTZ" SCHWARTZ
PRODUCTION EDITOR: CHRISTINE "STOLE MA HEART" MA

THE ILLUSTRATIONS FOR THIS BOOK WERE DONE IN ADOBE PHOTOSHOP.
THE TEXT WAS SET IN DANSANTAT, AND THE DISPLAY TYPE WAS HAND-LETTERED.

LITTLE, BROWN AND COMPANY
HACHETTE BOOK GROUP
1290 AVENUE OF THE AMERICAS, NEW YORK, NY 10104
VISIT US AT LB-KIDS.COM

LITTLE, BROWN AND COMPANY IS A DIVISION OF HACHETTE BOOK GROUP, INC.
THE LITTLE, BROWN NAME AND LOGO ARE TRADEMARKS OF HACHETTE BOOK
GROUP, INC.

THE PUBLISHER IS NOT RESPONSIBLE FOR WEBSITES (OR THEIR CONTENT)
THAT ARE NOT OWNED BY THE PUBLISHER.

FIRST EDITION: DECEMBER 2014

LIBRARY OF CONGRESS CATALOGING-IN-PUBLICATION DATA
BERGER, SAMANTHA.
A CRANKENSTEIN VALENTINE / WRITTEN BY SAMANTHA BERGER ;
ILLUSTRATED BY DAN SANTAT.—FIRST EDITION.   PAGES CM
SUMMARY: A BOY WHO LOOKS ORDINARY TRANSFORMS INTO GRUMBLING
CRANKENSTEIN ON THE MOST "LOVEY-DOVEY, YUCKIEST DAY OF THE YEAR."
ISBN 978-0-316-37638-9 (HARDCOVER)—
ISBN 978-0-316-25764-0 (EBOOK) [1. VALENTINE'S DAY—
FICTION. 2. MONSTERS—FICTION.] I. SANTAT, DAN,
ILLUSTRATOR. II. TITLE.   PZ7.B452136CU 2014
[E]—DC23   2014027062

10 9 8 7 6 5 4 3 2 1
WOR
PRINTED IN THE UNITED STATES OF AMERICA

A CRANKENSTEIN VALENTINE

WRITTEN BY
SAMANTHA BERGER

ILLUSTRATED BY
DAN SANTAT

LITTLE, BROWN AND COMPANY
NEW YORK • BOSTON

HAVE YOU SEEN MY LITTLE
SWEETHEART, CRANKENSTEIN?

YOU CAN'T *MISS* CRANKENSTEIN
ON VALENTINE'S DAY.

YOU WOULD SAY,
HAPPY VALENTINE'S DAY, MY LOVE!

CRANKENSTEIN WOULD SAY,

YECHHHH!

CRANKENSTEIN WOULD SAY,

YECHHHH!

YOU MIGHT SEE CRANKENSTEIN GETTING A BIG RED SMOOCH ON THE SCHOOL BUS.

YECHHHH!

OR EATING A HEART-SHAPED PEANUT BUTTER AND JELLY SANDWICH AND HEART-SHAPED APPLE SLICES...

AND USING A HEART-SHAPED NAPKIN—
COVERED IN HEARTS!

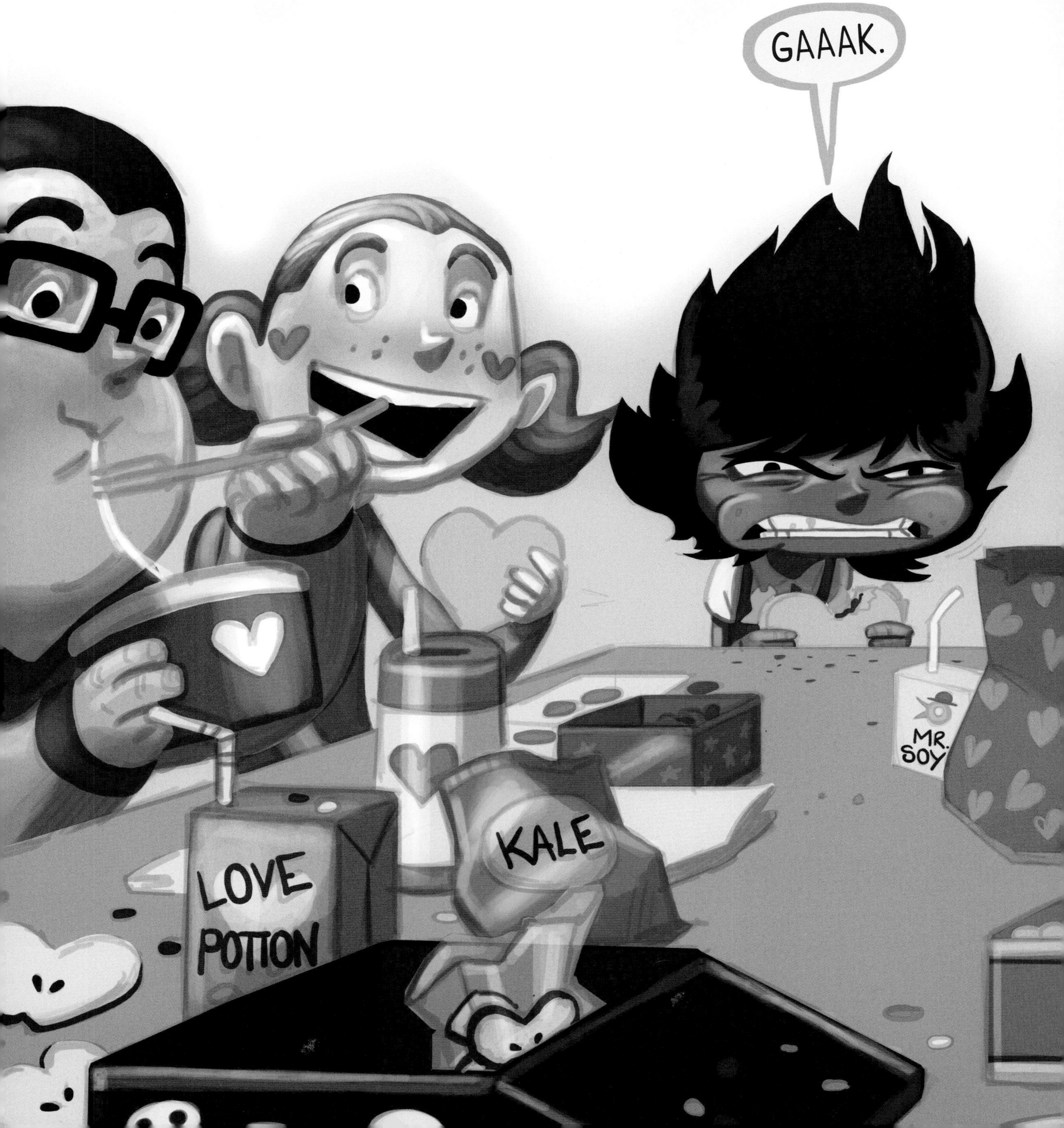

YOU COULD CERTAINLY FIND HIM BITING INTO A CHOCOLATE WITH SURPRISE HAIRY COCONUT INSIDE.

YECHHHH!

CRANKENSTEIN DOES NOT CARE
FOR THAT KIND OF CHOCOLATE.

OR HELPING TO MAKE THE MUSHY, GUSHY VALENTINE'S DAY GARLAND.

CRANKENSTEIN DOES NOT APPRECIATE HELPING TO MAKE THE MUSHY, GUSHY VALENTINE'S DAY GARLAND.

AND YOU'RE *GUARANTEED* TO FIND CRANKENSTEIN
IN THE VALENTINE'S DAY SCHOOL PAGEANT.

CRANKENSTEIN NEVER *SAID* HE WANTED TO BE
IN THE VALENTINE'S DAY SCHOOL PAGEANT.

NOPE, THERE'S ABSOLUTELY NO *WAY*, NO DOUBT, NOT NOW, NOT *EVER*, THAT CRANKENSTEIN WANTS ANYTHING TO DO WITH VALENTINE'S DAY!

A BEST FRIEND...

EXACTLY HOW YOU FEEL.
ROSES ARE RED.
VIOLETS ARE BLUE
ON VALENTINE'S DAY,
I FEEL JUST LIKE YOU!
EWWWW!

ONLY 364 DAYS UNTIL
NEXT VALENTINE'S DAY.